Hassan and Aneesa
Celebrate Eid

Yasmeen Rahim
Illustrated by Omar Burgess

Eid al-Fitr has started. The new moon has been seen and the special month of Ramadan is over.

Tomorrow, Mummy, Daddy, Hassan and Aneesa are having a party to celebrate Eid.

Everybody is helping to decorate the house. Hassan is looking for paper chains and Daddy hangs a banner. Mummy is blowing up balloons and Aneesa is trying to help. "My cheeks hurt," says Aneesa, all puffed out.

Mummy is cooking food for tomorrow. She is making salad, roast chicken and cake. "Aneesa, can you help me?" asks Mummy.

"OK," says Aneesa, "I'll try all the food for you."

Hassan is clearing the table and Daddy is hoovering the carpet. Soon the house is clean and a feast for all their friends and family is ready.

"Bedtime! We've got a busy day tomorrow," says Mummy.
Hassan and Aneesa are excited. They run upstairs and get ready for bed.

Mummy and Daddy have a few more jobs to do.

EID MUBARAK

Daddy wraps up Hassan and Aneesa's Eid presents.
They are a surprise. Afterwards he must pay Zakat-ul-Fitr.
It is money that helps the poor and needy.

It is the morning of Eid and everybody is in a hurry. The special Eid prayer starts soon. "We don't want to be late," says Daddy. Hassan has just showered. "I'm coming Daddy, wait for me," he says. "Aneesa, stop skipping and put your dress on," calls Mummy.

When everybody is dressed and ready to go they eat a date.

Hassan and Aneesa look smart in their Eid clothes.
They are on their way to the Eid prayer.
"Why are we going to the park?" asks Hassan.
"That is where we will pray," says Mummy. "The Prophet
Muhammad would perform the Eid prayer outside.
It is nice to follow his example."

Aneesa can hear lots of people up ahead. "What are they saying?" asks Aneesa. "They are saying the Eid takbir out loud before the prayer starts," says Daddy, "let's go and join them."

The Eid prayer has finished and everyone is sitting quietly. Only the imam is speaking.
"Allah likes it when we give money and food to poor and needy people. They should enjoy Eid too. We can also share food with friends, family and neighbours …"

Hassan listens carefully to the imam.

"Eid Mubarak!" Mummy says to Aneesa after the khutbah. "Eid Mubarak!" Aneesa replies with a big smile. "Let's find Daddy and Hassan, I want to say Eid Mubarak to them."

They walk across the park. It is bustling with people celebrating Eid. Mummy spots Hassan and waves. Daddy says goodbye to his friend. The party will start soon and they need to get home.

The doorbell rings.
"As-salamu 'alaykum.
Eid Mubarak!" says Daddy and
Mummy greeting their guests.

Hassan and Aneesa are in the living room.
They are busy unwrapping their presents.
"A pretty dolly, I love it," says Aneesa.
"Wow. My favourite game," says Hassan.

Soon the feast will be served. Everybody is in the garden waiting. Hassan is playing football and Daddy cooks food on the barbeque.

Aneesa is having fun skipping. She jumps faster and faster while Mummy talks to her friends.

It is getting late. All the guests say "as-salamu 'alaykum" and go home.
Mummy starts to tidy up. "There is plenty of Eid food left."
"Let's share it with our neighbours," Hassan says.
"That's a brilliant idea," replies Mummy.

Daddy knocks on Tom and Jemma's door.
"Hello, happy Eid, we have some food for you," says Daddy.
"This looks tasty. Thank you," says Tom.

Hassan and Aneesa have had a wonderful Eid…

... they don't want it to ever end.

Glossary

Allah: He is the one and only God that Muslims believe in.

As-salamu 'alaykum: "Peace be with you". A greeting Muslims say when they meet each other.

Eid al-Fitr: A Muslim festival. It is celebrated after the month of Ramadan has finished.

Eid Mubarak: "Happy Eid". A greeting people say to each other on Eid.

Eid Takbir: A prayer Muslims say aloud before the Eid prayer.

Imam: A Muslim man who leads the prayer.

Khutbah: A talk about Islam. It is given after the prayer on Eid.

Ramadan: A month in the Islamic calendar.

Zakat-ul-Fitr: Charity that is paid before the Eid prayer. It is used to give the poor and needy food on Eid.

Also available in the 'Hassan and Aneesa' series:

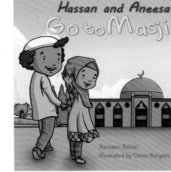

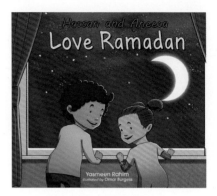

ISBN 978-0-86037-459-6   ISBN 978-0-86037-521-0   ISBN 978-0-86037-642-2

Hassan and Aneesa Celebrate Eid

Published by
THE ISLAMIC FOUNDATION
Markfield Conference Centre, Ratby Lane, Markfield,Leicestershire, LE67 9SY, United Kingdom
E-mail: publications@islamic-foundation.com Website: www.islamic-foundation.com

Qur'an House, P.O. BOX 30611, Nairobi, Kenya
P.M.B. 3193, Kano, Nigeria

Distributed by
KUBE PUBLISHING LTD
Tel +44 (01530) 249230 E-mail: info@kubepublishing.com Website: www.kubepublishing.com
7th impression, 2022.

Illustrations and cover art by Omar Burgess © Kube Publishing 2017
Book Design Nasir Cadir | *Editor* Yosef Smyth

ISBN 978-0-86037-698-9